PRESENTS

The Animal Shelf™

The Model Monster

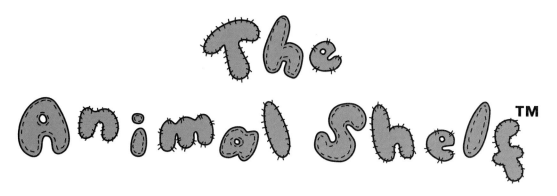

The Animal Shelf™

The Model Monster

Adapted by Sarah Heller

Based on *The Animal Shelf* created by Ivy Wallace

SCHOLASTIC INC.

New York   Toronto   London   Auckland   Sydney

Mexico City   New Delhi   Hong Kong   Buenos Aires

ISBN 0-439-31794-0

The Animal Shelf: Produced by Millimages SA and Zoo Lane Productions Ltd.™ and © 2001 Millimages SA/Zoo Lane Productions Ltd. Licensed by The itsy bitsy Entertainment Company.
Published by Scholastic Inc. SCHOLASTIC and associated logos are trademarks and/or registered trademarks of Scholastic Inc.

12 11 10 9 8 7 6 5 4 3 2 1   1 2 3 4 5 6/0

Printed in the U.S.A.
First Scholastic printing, December 2001

One day the Special Animals were busy planning what models to make for their friend Timothy. Stripey and Getup agreed to make a model house.

Gumpa the bear thought a plane would be great.

"No, let's make a robot," said Woeful.

Woeful took his boxes outside. He
looked at the pieces and imagined
his model.

It will be the world's greatest robot,
thought Woeful happily.

Little Mut helped Gumpa make a plane.

Stripey and Getup had just finished making their model house.

"It is a bit small," said Stripey.

Getup thought it would be the perfect house for Caterpillar.

In the garden, Caterpillar peeked through the window of his new house.

Oh, no! He saw a giant monster coming his way!

The monster was making scary noises.
The Special Animals ran to hide.

But Little Mut couldn't move. He'd been making a model with sticky tape and he was stuck to the front door.

Quickly, the animals pulled Little Mut free. They ran inside and slammed the door shut.

"It is only me!" cried Woeful on the other side of the door. He could not get out of his robot suit. Everyone was scared of him.

Quickly, the animals pulled Little Mut free. They ran inside and slammed the door shut.

"It is only me!" cried Woeful on the other side of the door. He could not get out of his robot suit. Everyone was scared of him.

In Timothy's bedroom, the animals made a plan to catch the monster. They took a pillowcase to the garden, but it started to rain.

The friends did not want to get wet. They waited inside for the rain to stop.

Where could Woeful be? they wondered.

Soon the sun came out. The animals saw the monster lying on the ground.

"I am not a monster!" Woeful cried to his friends. "I am Woeful!"

The Special Animals were surprised and happy to find their friend. There was no monster after all!

Woeful just laughed and laughed.

Finally, Timothy was home. But the animals were sad. Their models were ruined. Even the cardboard house had been eaten by Caterpillar.

Then the friends saw a new model. It was a car that Timothy had made for his Special Animals. This was the best surprise of all!

The End

We hope that you will enjoy all the
It's itsy bitsy Time! books:

The Animal Shelf: *The Model Monster*
Charley & Mimmo: *Learn Colors with Charley*
Charley & Mimmo: *Learn Numbers with Charley*
64 Zoo Lane: *Joey the Kangaroo*